The Waving Girl

The Waving Girl

By J. B. Nicholas

Illustrated by Joan C. Waites

PELICAN PUBLISHING COMPANY

Gretna 2004

*The word "Pelican" and the depiction of a pelican are trademarks
of Pelican Publishing Company, Inc., and are registered in the
U.S. Patent and Trademark Office.*

Library of Congress Cataloging-in-Publication Data

Nicholas, J. B. (Julie B.)
    The Waving Girl / by J.B. Nicholas ; illustrated by Joan C. Waites.
        p. cm.
    Summary: Relates the experiences of a girl who follows her lighthouse-keeper
father's advice to "be a light for others any way we can," and becomes world-famous
for waving at every boat passing Elba Isle, off the coast of Savannah, Georgia.
    ISBN 1-58980-185-7 (pbk. : alk. paper)
    [1. Martus, Florence—Fiction. 2. Lighthouse keepers—Fiction. 3. Neighborliness—
Fiction. 4. Statues—Fiction. 5. Islands—Fiction. 6. Savannah (Ga.)—Fiction.]   I.
Waites, Joan C., ill. II. Title.

    PZ7+
    [E]—dc22

                                                        2003027659

Printed in Singapore
Published by Pelican Publishing Company, Inc.
1000 Burmaster Street, Gretna, Louisiana 70053

THE WAVING GIRL

I am Flora of Elba Isle. On late summer afternoons I sit against the river's edge with Dandy and my brother, George. We breathe in the wind and water and watch ships pass to and from Savannah, a city that spills over with all sorts of people.

George works with Papa in the lighthouse. There are windows to wash, lanterns to light, and ships to log. Sometimes Papa lets me write a ship's name in the logbook.

Tonight I climb the lighthouse stairs with dinner. A beam of light shines over the black water, and my eyes follow a ship heading for Savannah.

"Papa," I say quietly, "I miss people."
Papa beckons for me to sit on his lap.
"Elba is only big enough for the lighthouse keeper,
Flora." I nod but say nothing. He points out the window.

"That beam of light guides ships to and from shore and warns them of danger. Sailors feel safe when they spot our Elba."

Papa waits a bit, then squeezes me tight, whispering in my ear, "We must always be a light for others any way we can."

On Friday we row our boat, *Cecelia,* into Savannah. While Papa and George shop for supplies, I visit my cousin, May.

Tucked in a row of fancy homes, May's house looks out over a square. We sit on a bench and watch people. It is like watching ships, but instead of sails and whistles, there are hats and voices.

"Hello, Mr. Murkle!" May waves to an older gentle-man.

"Good afternoon, May." He tips his hat as he passes.

"He's my neighbor," she whispers to me.

"Oh!" Wishing he would turn around, I stare at the back of Mr. Murkle. When he does, I shout, "Hello, Mr. Murkle!" and wave like May. He winks and tips his hat a second time. We giggle.

On the way home *Cecelia* rocks back and forth, but I
do not notice. I think about May and her neighbor and
feel a bit sad that I cannot live in a fancy house that
looks out over a square buzzing with neighbors.

But when I spot the lighthouse, my heart swells like the river. The strong beam of light makes me feel safe, and I think of Papa's words. *A light for others any way we can.*

Monday is shake-out day—shake out the blankets,
sheets, rugs, and lastly the apron tied around my waist.
Holding the apron high above my head, I stand on the
front porch and let the wind slap and billow the cotton.
Up and down my arms go.

A ship's whistle interrupts my thoughts. I look out
and see three figures waving something white from the
ship. What are they doing? I wonder.

Suddenly, I know. They are waving, saying hello
across the water. I wave my apron wildly up and down.
"Hello, neighbor," I whisper.

I can hardly wait for the next ship. Apron by day, lantern by night, I wave to each one. From Seattle to Singapore, word spreads. Sailors line the decks of ships as they near Savannah's shore to catch a glimpse of me waving.

I receive bags of letters and packages from around the world. Fruit, plants, jewelry, poems, and even exotic birds fill our home. They are all addressed to:

The Waving Girl
Elba Island, Georgia

But Papa shakes his head when Lady the llama arrives from Peru.

"Flora, Flora, wake up!"

It is the earliest hour one September morning when George wakes me. The howl of wind and rain outside muffles the moaning I hear from a bed in the corner. Am I dreaming?

"Papa fell down the stairs. I think he broke his leg," George explains as he hands me my cape. "There's a storm, Flora, and a boat's in trouble. Hurry! I'm going to need your help."

I take a deep breath and grab a lantern. The beacon lights are out. There is no time to light them.

While George struggles to row *Cecelia,* I sit at the bow and focus on the small boat ahead. I am trying hard to be brave, but my legs shake. Rain slices the air. The river is wild and choppy. Sharp wind steals my breath, and I am sure the lantern will go out.

When we finally reach the boat, a frightened fisherman is clinging to its side. His boat has flipped over. George and I pull him into our boat. He is shivering, so we wrap a blanket around him.

"Thank you," he whispers.

Cecelia pitches back and forth even more. I am sure we will tip over. My legs still shake, so I fix my eyes on the lantern, which is struggling to stay lit. Its light is comforting, and as we safely reach shore, Papa's words, strong and sure like the river, course through me. *A light for others any way we can.*

Many more ships come and go. Papa's leg is fine, but he limps from its ache. He squints to see at night, and wrinkles nest in the corners of his smile.

"It is time for George to run the lighthouse," Papa announces one evening.

My life is like a ship riding the river's current. Some days chug by so slowly I think they will never end. Others sail by pulling me along so strongly and swiftly I hardly remember them.

More ships come and go. George and I squint to see at night, and wrinkles nest in the corners of our smiles. It is time for someone else to run the lighthouse.

On a misty June morning I wave to one last ship and
tie my apron to the porch railing.
"Good-bye, neighbor," I whisper.

For my seventieth birthday, Savannah throws a party.
Three thousand people come with presents and the
biggest cake I have ever seen. I am not a speaker, so I
jot something down on a piece of paper and hand it to
the mayor. He stands and reads, "This is the grandest
day of my life."

I smile and nod. A child's clap breaks the quiet. Everyone stands to applaud. I close my eyes and let a river of tears stream down my weathered face.

Breathing in the faint smell of wind and water, I rise. Slowly, I pull a white hanky out of my pocket. Then up and down my arms go, waving once again.

I am Flora of Elba Isle. And deep inside me, Papa's
words still swell strong and sure like the river.

A light for others any way we can.